SHADOWS OF KIRIGAKURE

UTKARSH SINGH PATEL

Made with ❤ on the Notion Press Platform
www.notionpress.com

To the dreamers who dare to believe in light,
To the friends who stand by us in the darkest
times,
And to the heroes, big and small, who remind us
that courage lies within us all—
This story is for you.

Contents

Foreword

In the world of stories, some tales leave an imprint on your soul, and The Cave of Shadows and the Rise of Specter is one such journey. This book is not just a story about battles or ancient evil—it's about courage, teamwork, and the unbreakable bonds of friendship.

Set in the mysterious village of Kirigakure, this tale pulls you into a world of intrigue and danger, where young heroes rise to protect what matters most. As you follow Yamato and his friends, you'll see how even ordinary people can do extraordinary things when they stand together.

This book is perfect for readers who love adventure, mystery, and the thrill of facing the unknown. It reminds us that light shines brightest in the darkest moments. Open these pages, and prepare to embark on a journey you won't forget!

Preface

Above all, I would like to express my deepest gratitude to my family for their unwavering support throughout the writing process, .

Prologue

In the quiet village of Kirigakure, life was simple and peaceful. Surrounded by misty forests and tall mountains, the people believed they were safe from danger. But deep in the shadows of the land, an old darkness was waiting to return.

Long ago, an evil group called the Eternal Eclipse tried to cover the world in darkness. Led by powerful commanders, they destroyed everything in their path. It took brave warriors and ancient magic to stop them. The Eclipse was defeated, and its leaders were sealed away in hidden places. Over time, people forgot about the threat, thinking it was gone forever.

But darkness does not stay hidden for long.

When strange shadows started appearing in Kirigakure and the air became cold with whispers, the village's elder, Hiroshi, warned that the seals holding the darkness were weakening. A young swordsman named Yamato and his friends—Sana, Riku, Aiko, and Haru—were chosen to protect their home. They were brave, but they had no idea of the dangers ahead.

Their journey began in the Cave of Shadows, where they faced the Shadowbinder, one of the Eclipse's commanders. It was a terrifying battle, but the group worked together and used their courage and skills to seal the Shadowbinder once again. Though they won, they learned a chilling truth—the other commanders were awakening, and the worst was yet to come.

Not long after, another threat rose from the darkness. A new enemy, known as Specter, appeared. Unlike the Shadowbinder, Specter was cunning and clever, always staying one step ahead. As the group followed clues to stop this new villain, they realized they couldn't rely on strength alone. They would need wisdom, trust, and old alliances to survive.

The battle against darkness was far from over, and the fate of their world rested in their hands.

CHAPTER ONE

THE CAVE OF SHADOWS

In the village of Kirigakure, there was a cave high in the cliffs that everyone avoided. People said a scary creature lived inside, but Yamato didn't believe them. He thought there might be treasure hidden there, and he wanted to find it.

One afternoon, Yamato grabbed a lantern and a strong stick and climbed up to the cave. The path was steep, and the wind was cold, making the climb harder. When he reached the entrance, the cave looked dark and unwelcoming.

He lit his lantern and stepped inside. The air was cold and smelled strange, like metal and dirt. Shadows from the lantern flickered on the walls, making the cave look alive. The ground was uneven, and the walls seemed to close in the deeper he went.

As he walked, he saw strange markings on the walls. They looked like symbols, but Yamato didn't know what they meant. The air felt heavier, and the silence made his footsteps sound louder. He told himself he wasn't scared, but his hands gripped the stick tightly.

Then he heard it.

A low, deep growl came from the darkness ahead. Yamato froze. The growl came again, louder this time. He raised his lantern and saw two glowing yellow eyes staring at him.

The creature stepped into the light. It was big, covered in dark, shiny scales, with sharp claws that scratched the cave floor. It growled, and Yamato felt his chest shake from the sound.

Without thinking, Yamato turned and ran. The creature roared and chased after him, its heavy steps shaking the ground. Yamato's lantern swung wildly as he ran, lighting up the jagged rocks around him.

He knew he couldn't outrun it. The cave was too small, and the creature was too fast. Then he saw a loose rock leaning against the wall. Using all his strength, Yamato pushed it over. The rock fell, blocking part of the path.

The creature roared and clawed at the rock, but Yamato didn't wait to see if it would get through. He kept running toward the entrance.

Just as he reached the mouth of the cave, the creature lunged again. Its claws grazed his back, but Yamato managed to dive outside and roll onto the rocky ground.

Breathing hard, he looked back at the cave. The creature had stopped chasing him. It stood in the shadows, its glowing eyes watching him before it turned and disappeared into the darkness.

Yamato sat on the ground, shaking. He didn't find treasure, but he had found the creature—and now he wished he had stayed far away from the cave.

Yamato lay on the rocky ground, his heart still racing. He couldn't believe what had just happened. The creature had been so close. He could still feel the cold air from its breath on his back. The thought of going back into the cave made him shudder.

But he couldn't just leave it like that. The creature had scared him, but he couldn't help but feel like there was something important about the cave. The markings on the walls, the creature itself—there was more to this place than just danger.

Yamato stood up slowly, his legs shaky. His lantern still flickered in his hand. He turned to look back at the cave. The entrance looked dark and empty now, almost peaceful. But deep down, he knew the creature was still there, somewhere in the shadows.

He glanced around. The cliffside was quiet, too quiet. The wind had stopped, and the sky above was heavy with dark clouds. Yamato took a deep breath. He didn't want to go back into the cave. But he had to know what was inside.

With a quick glance behind him to make sure the creature wasn't following, Yamato crept toward the cave entrance again. This time, he was more careful, more aware of every sound around him. The air was colder as he stepped back into the darkness, but his lantern cast a steady light now, pushing the shadows away.

The cave seemed to stretch out longer than it had before. Yamato moved cautiously, the floor crunching beneath his feet as he walked. The strange symbols on the walls looked even more mysterious now, almost as if they were glowing faintly in the lantern light.

He reached the spot where he had dropped the rock earlier. It was still in place, blocking part of the path. Yamato bent down and peered around the rock, his eyes adjusting to the dark. There, in the distance, he saw something that made his heart skip a beat: a faint blue light flickering in the darkness.

It wasn't the creature's eyes this time. It was a soft, steady glow, like a lantern but brighter, pulsing with an energy that seemed almost alive. Yamato moved toward it, his breath coming faster now.

As he got closer, the light grew stronger, and the air around him began to hum. He reached out a hand, hesitating for a moment before touching the stone wall beside the glowing light. The moment his fingers made contact, the hum grew louder, almost like a whisper, soft but clear.

"Leave... now."

Yamato's heart raced, and he pulled his hand back, looking around in a panic. The voice wasn't the creature's—it was something else, something far older and colder. The light flickered again, then faded.

A shadow moved from the corner of his eye. Yamato spun around, his stick raised, but he couldn't see anything. The cave felt suddenly alive with movement, as if the walls themselves were watching him.

Then, from the very back of the cave, he heard a noise: a low, deep growl, but this one wasn't from the creature. It came from deeper inside, beyond where the light had been. The sound echoed off the walls, shaking Yamato to his core.

The growl was followed by a loud cracking sound. The ground beneath his feet trembled, and the cave seemed to shift, as if it was alive, breathing.

Yamato backed up, his lantern swinging wildly. He had to get out. The path behind him was blocked by rocks, and ahead was the deep, dark unknown.

Then, something caught his eye. A narrow passageway he hadn't seen before, hidden in the shadows. It wasn't much of a choice—he had to run.

Yamato darted toward the passage, squeezing through the narrow opening just as the growl turned into a roar. The creature was getting closer. The walls of the cave were shaking now, and the air felt thick with the energy that had awakened.

He crawled through the passage, his hands scraping against the rough stone. The roar of the creature echoed behind him, but he kept moving, faster and faster.

Finally, the passage opened into a larger chamber. It was dark, but there was something in the center of the room that caught his attention—a strange stone pedestal, glowing faintly in the dark. On top of the pedestal was an old, dusty book, its pages yellowed with age.

Yamato approached it cautiously, his fingers trembling as he reached for the book. Just as his hand brushed against it, he heard a voice—clearer now, colder, and unmistakably not human.

"You should not have come..."

The book's cover snapped open on its own, and the ground beneath Yamato's feet trembled once more. The cave seemed to groan, like a giant waking from a long sleep.

Yamato's heart raced as the air grew colder. He had to leave, but the book... the creature... and the whispers were all closing in. The cave wasn't just a place of darkness—it was a prison. And now, it was awake.

Yamato's fingers trembled as he held the ancient book. The cold voice that echoed through the cave sent chills down his spine, and the ground beneath him continued to shake. He looked around the dark chamber, his eyes darting from the glowing book to the narrow passageway he had crawled through.

But then, the tremors stopped. The cave fell silent again, and for a moment, Yamato thought it was over. Maybe he had imagined the voice. But when he turned to look back, the narrow passage he had entered through was no longer visible. The walls of the cave seemed to have shifted, sealing him in.

Yamato's heart pounded as he looked around for another way out. That's when he heard voices.

"Yamato!" came a shout from behind him.

He spun around, and to his surprise, three figures appeared from the darkness. It was his friends—Riku, Aiko, and Haru—who had been following him since he left the village. Yamato had no idea they had been so close.

"Are you okay?" Riku asked, his voice full of worry as he stepped into the light. He was carrying a sword, the hilt wrapped tightly in his hand.

"Not exactly," Yamato replied, his voice strained. He pointed to the book in his hands. "This... this is what I found."

Aiko, who was the fastest and most agile of their group, quickly scanned the room. "We need to get out of here, Yamato. The cave feels... wrong. Like it's alive."

"I tried to leave, but the way is blocked," Yamato said, his eyes flicking nervously to the walls, still vibrating with energy.

Haru, the quietest of the group but the most practical, stepped closer to the pedestal and crouched down to examine the book. "We can't just leave. Whatever this book is, it's tied to whatever is happening here." He reached out to touch it, but Yamato pulled it away, suddenly protective of the object.

"You don't understand," Yamato said quickly. "I heard a voice... something dark. I think it's part of the curse that controls this cave."

At that moment, the ground trembled again, much stronger this time. The walls groaned as if they were waking up. A low, echoing growl resonated from deep within the cave, sending a wave of fear through all of them. The growl was closer than before.

"We need to move now!" Aiko shouted. "That thing's coming!"

The group turned to run, but just as they made their way to the far side of the chamber, a massive shadow appeared. The creature from earlier stepped into the chamber, its glowing yellow eyes gleaming in the dark. It was larger than before, its jagged claws scraping against the stone floor as it advanced toward them.

"Move!" Riku yelled, drawing his sword and rushing forward. The creature swiped at him with terrifying speed, but Riku blocked the strike with his sword just in time. The force of the blow sent him tumbling backward, but he quickly got back to his feet.

"Aiko, Haru—get Yamato out of here!" Riku commanded, his sword raised in defense.

"No way," Aiko protested, her fists clenched in determination. "We stick together."

"We don't have time for this!" Haru said urgently. "If we don't move now, we'll all be trapped!"

Haru pulled Yamato away from the pedestal and pushed him toward a nearby tunnel that had been hidden in the shadows. Yamato hesitated, the book still clutched in his hand. He wanted to help Riku, but he knew there was nothing they could do against that creature—not in this cave, not without a plan.

As they ran, the creature roared, shaking the cave with its fury. Aiko and Haru led the way, moving fast through the narrow tunnel. Yamato's heart raced in his chest, the growls of the creature fading behind them, but still present in the air, like a shadow hunting them.

They ran for what felt like hours, the tunnel winding deeper into the cave. The walls felt like they were closing in, and the air grew thick and suffocating. Yamato didn't know how long they had been running when they finally reached a small chamber. It was cold and empty, save for another stone pedestal, this one much older, covered in moss.

"We need to hide," Aiko said, panting for breath.

They huddled together in the far corner, trying to catch their breath and plan their next move. Yamato gripped the book tightly, his mind racing with thoughts of what they had just seen. The creature, the whispers, the shifting cave—it was clear that something much darker was controlling everything.

"We can't keep running," Haru said, his voice calm but serious. "We need to destroy whatever is causing this. The creature, the curse—it's all tied to the book. We can't let it fall into the wrong hands."

"Right," Yamato agreed. "But we need a plan."

As they discussed their next move, the sound of footsteps echoed through the chamber. The growls had stopped, but something much more chilling had taken its place: a soft, whistling noise, like the wind passing through a crack. And then, a low voice that chilled Yamato to his bones.

"You should never have come..."

The voice echoed through the room again, and the shadows seemed to stretch, swirling around them as if the cave itself was coming to life.

Yamato looked around, realizing that they were no longer alone.

The whispers were growing louder. The creature wasn't the only danger they had to face anymore. Something darker, something ancient, was watching them now.

The voice echoed again, the words hanging in the air like a warning, and the shadows seemed to stretch even further, closing in around them. Yamato's heart pounded in his chest as the cold air grew heavier, pressing against his skin. His eyes flicked nervously between his friends. They were just as tense, if not more so.

Aiko gripped her fists tighter, her usual confidence replaced by uncertainty. "What was that?" she whispered, her eyes scanning the darkness.

Haru, ever calm but clearly on edge, lowered his head as if listening to the very walls themselves. "It's not just the creature anymore," he said softly. "There's something else. Something older."

Yamato felt the weight of those words settle over him like a heavy cloak. This wasn't just some cave. It was a prison. A place where something dark had been sealed away for ages—and now, they had disturbed it.

Before they could speak again, the ground trembled beneath their feet. The walls groaned, as if something deep within the cave was stirring, awakening from its long sleep. The soft whistling noise turned into a low, eerie hum. Yamato felt the vibration in his bones, and a cold sweat trickled down his neck.

"Move!" Haru shouted, snapping everyone into action.

They bolted for the entrance of the chamber, but just as they reached it, the path they had taken before was blocked by a thick, swirling fog. The air around them grew heavier, colder, and the light from Yamato's lantern flickered as if struggling to stay alive.

The fog pressed in on them, swallowing everything in its path. Yamato couldn't see more than a few feet ahead, but he could feel the presence of something watching them—something ancient and powerful.

The creature's roar echoed again, but it sounded different now. It was distant, almost as if it was being dragged back into the darkness, forced into the depths of the cave.

"Keep moving!" Aiko urged, grabbing Yamato's arm and pulling him through the mist.

They stumbled through the fog, disoriented and unsure of which way to go. The whispers grew louder, swirling around them like a storm. It felt like the cave was alive—its walls closing in, the ground shifting beneath them.

Yamato could barely keep his balance, his breath shallow and quick, his thoughts scattered. "What do we do now?!" he asked, his voice cracking.

"We need to find the source of the power," Haru said urgently, his eyes darting around the mist. "Whatever that book is, it's tied to this place. If we can destroy it, maybe we can stop whatever is causing this."

Yamato gripped the book tighter, his hand trembling. The whispers were growing louder now, and the shadows were pressing in on them from all sides.

Then, from the heart of the fog, a figure emerged. It was tall and cloaked in darkness, its face hidden in shadow. The figure was unlike anything they had seen before—part human, part something else. It radiated an unsettling power that made Yamato's blood run cold.

The figure spoke, its voice low and smooth, but with an edge of anger. "You should never have come. The cave is no longer just a prison. It is my domain, and now, you are trapped within it."

Yamato's heart skipped a beat. "Who are you?" he demanded, though his voice trembled. "What do you want?"

The figure stepped forward, its presence suffocating. The fog seemed to part around it as if it was the source of the mist itself. "I am the Keeper of the Cave," it said, its voice reverberating through Yamato's mind. "And you have unleashed that which should remain sealed. The creature, the book, and the curse are all parts of me."

Yamato's eyes widened. The Keeper? The curse? The creature? It was all connected.

The Keeper raised its hand, and the mist thickened again, swirling violently around them. "You have three choices," it intoned, its voice echoing like thunder. "One, you leave the cave and never return. Two, you face the creature and try to defeat it. Or three... you join me. Forever."

Aiko took a step forward, her eyes fierce. "We're not afraid of you," she said, though her voice wavered slightly. "We'll destroy the book. Whatever you are, you won't control us."

The Keeper's laugh was cold, a sound that seemed to chill the very air. "You think the book is the key?" it scoffed. "The book is nothing but a tool. The true power lies in what you've awakened."

Before they could react, the ground beneath them split open, and a massive hand, covered in scales and glowing with an otherworldly light, shot out from the ground. The creature—the one they had thought was far away—was here, and it was enormous.

Yamato's heart pounded in his chest as the creature let out a deafening roar, its glowing eyes fixed on them. The Keeper's power was flowing through it, and it was more terrifying than Yamato had ever imagined.

"We need to destroy the book NOW!" Haru shouted.

But before they could even move, the Keeper's hand shot out, grabbing the book from Yamato's hands. The creature's eyes flared with a sudden burst of energy, and the entire cave seemed to tremble with power.

The Keeper held the book high above its head. "The game is over," it said with a cold smile. "You have lost."

Yamato, Aiko, Haru, and Riku stood frozen, watching as the cave seemed to come alive around them, and they realized—this was just the beginning. The Keeper had unleashed its full power, and they were trapped.

The only question left was whether they would survive long enough to stop it.

The air was thick with an unnatural energy as the Keeper held the glowing book above its head, a sinister smile spreading across its shadowed face. The creature beside it snarled, its massive claws carving deep grooves into the cave floor. The walls trembled, and the whispers turned into a deafening roar, like the cave itself was crying out in pain.

Yamato's mind raced. They were out of options, cornered by forces far beyond anything they'd ever encountered. Aiko clenched her fists, her face pale but resolute. Haru was scanning the chamber, his sharp eyes searching for anything they could use, and Riku tightened his grip on his sword, his jaw set in defiance.

"We can't let this thing win!" Aiko yelled over the chaos.

"But how?" Yamato shouted back. "The book... the creature... it's too much!"

"It's always been about the book!" Haru said, his voice cutting through the noise. "Destroy it, and we might have a chance!"

The Keeper's laughter echoed once again, its voice mocking and cold. "Fools," it said, its tone dripping with disdain. "This book is no longer yours to destroy. Its power feeds me now, and through it, I shall escape this prison and consume your world."

Riku stepped forward, determination blazing in his eyes. "Not if we stop you first!" He charged at the Keeper, his sword flashing as he swung it with all his strength. The blade struck the Keeper's shadowy form, but instead of cutting through, it passed harmlessly, as though slicing through smoke.

The Keeper raised its hand, and Riku was thrown backward by an invisible force, crashing into the wall with a grunt of pain. Aiko rushed to help him, but the creature lunged forward, blocking her path with a swipe of its massive claws.

Haru grabbed Yamato's arm, pulling him back. "Yamato, listen to me! The Keeper might be invincible, but the book isn't. We need to destroy it before it fully merges with that thing!"

"But how?" Yamato asked, desperation rising in his voice.

Haru looked at the glowing pedestal where the book had originally rested. "The pedestal! It must be linked to the book's power. If we can sever that connection—"

A sudden roar cut him off as the creature charged toward them, its glowing eyes locked onto Yamato. Time seemed to slow as the massive beast lunged, its claws poised to strike.

"Move!" Aiko shouted, tackling Yamato out of the way just in time. The creature's claws slammed into the ground, sending cracks spiderwebbing through the floor.

Riku, bruised but still determined, scrambled to his feet. He gripped his sword tightly and yelled, "Keep it distracted! I'll go for the pedestal!"

The others nodded, splitting up to draw the creature's attention. Aiko darted to the left, throwing small rocks to distract the beast, while Haru moved to the right, shouting and waving his arms. The creature roared in frustration, its movements slower now as it tried to track them all at once.

Meanwhile, Riku sprinted toward the pedestal, his eyes locked on the glowing base. He reached it and raised his sword, ready to strike, but the Keeper turned toward him, its shadowy form surging forward.

"You dare defy me?" the Keeper roared, its voice shaking the chamber. With a wave of its hand, tendrils of darkness shot out, wrapping around Riku's legs and dragging him to the ground.

"Riku!" Yamato shouted, his heart pounding.

Without thinking, Yamato charged toward the Keeper. He had no weapon, no plan, just raw determination. As the shadows closed in around Riku, Yamato grabbed a jagged piece of broken rock from the ground and hurled it at the Keeper with all his strength.

The rock struck the book, and for a brief moment, the glowing symbols on its surface flickered. The Keeper let out a furious roar, its grip on Riku faltering.

"Yamato, again!" Haru yelled.

Yamato didn't hesitate. He grabbed another rock and threw it, this time aiming directly for the book. The impact sent a shockwave through the chamber, and the glowing light on the pedestal dimmed.

The Keeper shrieked, its shadowy form twisting and writhing. "No! You cannot—"

Before it could finish, Aiko leapt onto the pedestal, her eyes blazing with determination. She reached out, grabbed the book, and slammed it down onto the pedestal with all her might. The glowing light flared brightly, then shattered like glass.

A deafening roar filled the chamber as the Keeper and the creature both howled in pain. The shadows around them began to dissolve, melting into the air like mist under the morning sun.

The ground shook violently, and cracks spread across the walls and ceiling. "The cave is collapsing!" Haru shouted.

"Run!" Riku yelled, pulling himself to his feet.

The group bolted toward the nearest tunnel, the cave crumbling around them. Stones fell from above, and the air was filled with dust and debris. Yamato led the way, the dim light of his lantern guiding them through the chaos.

Just as they reached the entrance, the final roar of the Keeper echoed behind them, followed by a blinding flash of light. The force of the explosion propelled them out of the cave and onto the rocky cliffside, where they collapsed in a heap.

For a long moment, no one spoke. They lay there, gasping for breath, their bodies aching but alive. When Yamato finally looked back, the cave entrance was gone, buried beneath a mountain of rubble.

"It's over," Haru said quietly, his voice filled with relief.

Yamato sat up, his hands still trembling. He glanced at the others, their faces streaked with dirt but glowing with triumph. For the first time in hours, the air felt clear, free of the oppressive weight of the cave's curse.

But as he looked out at the horizon, Yamato couldn't shake the feeling that their victory had come at a price. The Keeper might be gone, but the secrets of the cave—and the power they had unleashed—would never truly be forgotten.

The battle was over, but the shadows lingered. And deep in his heart, Yamato knew their story wasn't finished yet.

The Shadows That Remain

Days passed since the cave's collapse, but the events inside lingered in Yamato's mind like a storm refusing to settle. Back in Kirigakure, life resumed its usual rhythm, but for Yamato, Aiko, Riku, and Haru, nothing felt the same.

Yamato often found himself staring at the mountains that concealed the now-buried cave. Every gust of wind that swept through the village carried with it a faint, haunting echo—an echo he couldn't be sure wasn't just his imagination. He had thought they had sealed the curse, destroyed the book, and defeated the Keeper, but a shadow of unease remained.

One evening, as the village prepared for a festival to celebrate the harvest, Yamato met with the others near the old training grounds. It was their usual meeting spot, a quiet clearing surrounded by tall, swaying trees.

"We need to talk," Yamato said, his voice low but firm.

Riku, leaning against a tree with his arms crossed, raised an eyebrow. "About what? We won, didn't we? The cave's gone, the Keeper's gone. What's left to worry about?"

"That's the problem," Yamato replied. "I don't think it's over."

Aiko, sitting on a low branch, tilted her head. "What do you mean? We destroyed the book. That thing can't come back without it."

Haru, who had been silent until now, spoke up, his tone thoughtful. "Yamato might be right. The book was just a vessel for the Keeper's power, but the Keeper itself wasn't truly destroyed. It was trapped in the cave, and we only managed to seal it in again. What if it finds another way out?"

The group fell silent, the weight of Haru's words sinking in.

"It's more than that," Yamato said, clenching his fists. "Since we left the cave, I've been... feeling something. Like it's still watching us. I've had dreams—visions—of the Keeper. It's like it's trying to reach out to me."

Aiko hopped down from the branch, her expression serious now. "If that's true, then we can't ignore it. What do you think it wants?"

"I don't know," Yamato admitted. "But I think it's connected to us somehow. Maybe because we were the ones who broke the seal in the first place."

Before anyone could respond, a sharp crack echoed through the clearing. The group froze, their eyes darting toward the source of the sound. It came from the woods, just beyond the training grounds.

Riku unsheathed his sword, his muscles tensing. "Stay alert. It could be anything—or anyone."

The group moved cautiously toward the sound, their senses heightened. As they approached the edge of the woods, a figure stepped out from the shadows. It was a young girl, no older than twelve, with pale skin and long, dark hair that seemed to shimmer in the moonlight. She wore a tattered cloak, and her eyes—wide and unnervingly bright—locked onto Yamato.

"You've seen it, haven't you?" she said, her voice soft but haunting.

Yamato took a step back, his heart pounding. "Seen what?"

"The Keeper," she replied, her gaze never leaving his. "It's not gone. You've only made it angry."

The others exchanged uneasy glances, but Yamato stepped forward, his voice steady despite his fear. "Who are you? How do you know about the Keeper?"

The girl tilted her head, a small, sad smile on her lips. "Because it's been following me, too. Ever since I touched the first seal. I thought I could escape it, but it always finds a way back."

Haru frowned. "First seal? What do you mean? Are there more caves like the one we found?"

The girl nodded slowly. "The Keeper's prison wasn't just one cave. It's connected to others, scattered across the land. Each one holds a piece of its power. You destroyed one, but the others are still out there. And now that you've awakened it, it won't rest until it's whole again."

The weight of her words hit them like a thunderclap. The Keeper wasn't just a single entity; it was a force tied to multiple places, each one holding a fragment of its strength.

"What do we do?" Aiko asked, her voice barely above a whisper.

The girl's gaze darkened. "You have to find the other seals before the Keeper does. If it gathers all its power, not even the strongest warriors will be able to stop it."

Riku stepped forward, his jaw tight. "Why should we believe you? For all we know, you could be working with it."

The girl's eyes flashed with anger. "I'm not working with it! I've been running from it my whole life. I came here because I sensed its power awakening—and because you're the only ones who can stop it now."

Yamato looked into her eyes, searching for any hint of deceit, but all he saw was fear. She was telling the truth.

"What's your name?" he asked gently.

The girl hesitated before answering. "Sana," she said. "And if we don't act fast, we're all going to regret it."

The group stood in silence, the gravity of their situation sinking in. The Keeper wasn't defeated—it was gathering strength, and they were the only ones who could stop it.

Yamato took a deep breath, his resolve hardening. "Then we have no choice. We find the other seals and destroy them, no matter what it takes."

The others nodded, their expressions grim but determined.

The fight wasn't over. It had only just begun.

The Keeper's Hunt

The night deepened as Sana led Yamato and the group toward the edge of Kirigakure. Her movements were swift and sure, as though she had traveled these woods many times before. The forest was eerily silent, save for the crunch of leaves under their feet. It felt like the world itself was holding its breath, waiting for what would come next.

Yamato couldn't shake the weight of her words. The Keeper wasn't just trapped; it was gathering strength, and it was up to them to stop it. Sana had said there were other seals, scattered across the land, each tied to the Keeper's power. He glanced at his friends. Riku was tense but ready, gripping his sword like it was an extension of himself. Aiko kept her focus ahead, her fists clenched and steady. Haru moved quietly, his eyes scanning the shadows, always thinking two steps ahead.

They emerged from the trees into a rocky clearing. In the center stood the ruins of an old shrine, overgrown with moss and vines. The air here was heavy, and Yamato felt a strange chill crawl up his spine.

"This is where it begins," Sana said, stepping forward. She pointed to the shrine. "Inside, there's an artifact. It will show us where the other seals are."

Riku stepped closer, his eyes narrowing. "How do you know all this? You seem to know more about the Keeper than you're letting on."

Sana hesitated, her gaze dropping to the ground. "I told you—I've been running from it for years. I found one of the seals when I was a child. Ever since then, I've been tied to it, just like you are now. If you want to survive, you have to trust me."

Before anyone could respond, the ground beneath them trembled. A low rumble echoed through the clearing, and the air grew colder. The faint whispers Yamato remembered from the cave returned, growing louder with each passing moment.

"It's here," Haru said, his voice barely above a whisper.

The shadows around the shrine began to twist and move as if alive. From the darkness, a familiar figure emerged—the Keeper's form, fragmented and incomplete, but no less menacing. Its eyes glowed like embers, and its voice echoed in their minds.

"You thought you could escape me," it said, its tone dripping with malice. "But I am eternal. You cannot destroy what I am."

The group drew their weapons, forming a defensive circle around Sana. The Keeper didn't attack immediately. Instead, it loomed over them, its shadowy tendrils reaching out, probing, testing.

"Go!" Yamato shouted to Sana. "Get the artifact!"

Sana hesitated for a moment, then sprinted toward the shrine. The Keeper roared, its form shifting violently as it lunged toward her. Yamato stepped in its path, slashing at the shadow with his blade. The Keeper recoiled, its form rippling like smoke, but the force of its counterattack sent Yamato sprawling.

"Hold it off!" Riku yelled, charging at the creature. His sword flashed as he struck, each blow forcing the Keeper back, but the effort was draining. The Keeper's form seemed endless, every slash met with more shadow pouring forth.

Aiko darted around the creature, striking its tendrils with quick, precise blows. "We can't keep this up forever!" she shouted. "Sana, hurry!"

Inside the shrine, Sana reached the central altar. A faint glow emanated from within, and she carefully pushed aside the moss and rubble to reveal a small, intricately carved orb. As her fingers touched it, the whispers stopped abruptly, replaced by a deafening silence.

The Keeper screamed, its form convulsing. "No! You will not take it from me!"

The creature surged forward, abandoning its fight with Yamato and the others. In an instant, it was at the entrance of the shrine, its tendrils crashing against an invisible barrier that shimmered faintly around Sana.

Yamato staggered to his feet, his body aching but his resolve unbroken. "We won't let you have her!" he shouted, rushing forward.

The group launched a desperate assault, their attacks coordinated and relentless. Haru hurled stones from a slingshot, aiming for the Keeper's glowing eyes, while Riku and Aiko struck its shifting form with everything they had.

Sana emerged from the shrine, clutching the glowing orb tightly. "I have it!" she cried. "But we have to go now!"

The Keeper let out an ear-splitting roar, its form growing larger and more chaotic. The shadows around it lashed out violently, striking the ground and trees, leaving destruction in their wake.

Haru grabbed Sana's arm. "This way!" he yelled, leading her toward the path back to the village. The others followed, the Keeper in furious pursuit.

The forest became a blur as they ran, the glowing orb in Sana's hands lighting their way. The Keeper's presence loomed behind them, its voice echoing through the trees. "You cannot escape me! You are mine!"

As they reached the outskirts of Kirigakure, Yamato turned to face the creature one last time. He raised his sword, his hands trembling but his heart resolute. "We'll stop you," he said, his voice steady despite the fear coursing through him. "No matter what it takes."

The Keeper hesitated, its form flickering as though weakened. Its glowing eyes fixed on the orb in Sana's hands, and for a moment, it seemed to withdraw.

"This is far from over," it said, its voice cold and venomous. With that, it melted into the shadows, vanishing into the night.

The group stood in silence, their breaths ragged. Sana held the orb close, her face pale but determined.

"We have what we need," she said. "But the fight is only beginning."

Yamato looked at his friends, their faces weary but filled with the same resolve that burned within him. The Keeper was still out there, and the seals remained. Their journey was far from over.

The Keeper's Vengeance

The night was quiet once more, but the group knew it was only a brief reprieve. Back in Kirigakure, they gathered in Yamato's home, where Sana carefully placed the glowing orb on the wooden table. Its faint light cast shifting patterns on the walls, and the air around it buzzed with an otherworldly energy.

"This is the key," Sana said, her voice steady despite the exhaustion etched into her face. "It doesn't just show where the seals are—it can activate them. Each seal can trap a fragment of the Keeper's power. If we can find them all, we can contain it completely."

Yamato stared at the orb, his mind racing. "But we don't even know where the other seals are yet. How do we find them before the Keeper does?"

Sana pointed to the orb. "This will guide us. It reacts to the presence of the Keeper's power. When we get close to another seal, it will glow brighter."

Haru frowned, leaning against the wall. "That's a solid plan, but there's one problem. The Keeper knows we have the orb now. It'll come for us the moment we leave the village."

Riku, sharpening his sword in the corner, smirked. "Let it come. We'll be ready."

Aiko crossed her arms, her expression serious. "This isn't just about fighting it off. The Keeper gets stronger every time it appears. If we don't move fast, we won't stand a chance."

Sana nodded. "We leave at dawn. The nearest seal is in the mountains to the north. It's the most dangerous one to reach, but it's also the closest."

The group exchanged determined glances. They were battered, scared, and unsure of what lay ahead, but they had come too far to back down now.

By sunrise, they were on the move. The orb, safely wrapped in cloth, hung from Sana's belt, its faint glow guiding their path. The northern mountains loomed in the distance, their jagged peaks shrouded in mist. The trek was grueling, the terrain steep and unforgiving, but the group pressed on, driven by the knowledge of what was at stake.

As they climbed higher, the air grew colder, and the landscape turned barren. The whispers returned, faint at first but growing louder with each step. The Keeper's presence was near.

Suddenly, the ground beneath them trembled. Rocks tumbled down the mountainside, and a low, guttural growl echoed through the valley. From the shadows of the cliffs, the Keeper emerged. This time, its form was larger, more solid, and more menacing. Its eyes burned with fury as it loomed over them.

"You think you can outrun me?" it hissed, its voice reverberating through the air. "You are fools. This power will be mine, and you will bow before me."

Yamato drew his sword, his heart pounding. "We won't let you win."

The Keeper lunged, its shadowy tendrils slicing through the air. The group scattered, each of them moving with practiced precision. Riku charged forward, his blade flashing as he struck at the creature's core. Aiko followed, her movements quick and agile as she landed blow after blow.

Haru stayed back, using his slingshot to aim at the Keeper's glowing eyes. Each hit made it recoil slightly, but the creature seemed more resilient than before.

Sana knelt on the ground, clutching the orb. "I can activate the seal," she shouted, her voice strained. "But I need time!"

Yamato nodded, positioning himself between Sana and the Keeper. "We'll hold it off!"

The battle was fierce. The Keeper's attacks were relentless, each strike shaking the ground and sending shockwaves through the air. Yamato and Riku fought side by side, their blades flashing as they parried and countered the creature's attacks. Aiko darted around its flanks, landing precise hits that disrupted its form. Haru's sharp eyes and quick reflexes kept the group from being overwhelmed.

But the Keeper was learning. Its movements grew faster, more coordinated, and its tendrils lashed out with deadly precision. It struck the ground near Aiko, sending her tumbling. Haru barely pulled her to safety in time.

"We can't keep this up!" Riku shouted, his breaths ragged.

Behind them, the orb began to glow brighter, its light intensifying until it was almost blinding. Sana's voice rang out, clear and commanding. "The seal is ready! Get back!"

The group scrambled away as the ground beneath the Keeper erupted with light. A circle of ancient symbols appeared, glowing with the same eerie energy as the orb. The Keeper roared, its form writhing as the light consumed it.

"This isn't over!" it screamed, its voice filled with rage and desperation. "You cannot stop me! I will return!"

With a final, deafening roar, the Keeper's form was sucked into the seal. The light faded, and the symbols etched themselves into the rock, glowing faintly before disappearing.

The group stood in stunned silence, their breaths heavy. Sana held the orb tightly, its glow now faint but steady.

"That's one seal down," she said, her voice shaking but resolute. "But there are still more to go."

Yamato looked at his friends, their faces a mix of relief and determination. The battle had taken its toll, but they were alive—and they had won a small but crucial victory.

"We'll find the others," Yamato said, his voice steady. "And we'll finish this, no matter what it takes."

As the group began their descent from the mountains, the whispers faded, replaced by the sound of the wind. But in the back of Yamato's mind, he knew the Keeper's words were more than a threat. It was still out there, watching, waiting.

The fight was far from over, but for now, they had hope—and that was enough to keep them going.

The Keeper's Fury

The group descended from the mountain, their breaths heavy and their bodies aching. The glowing orb in Sana's hands was now dim, its energy depleted from activating the seal. Despite the exhaustion, there was a flicker of hope among them. They had defeated the Keeper, albeit temporarily, and activated the first seal.

But the weight of the journey ahead loomed over them like a storm cloud. Sana had said there were multiple seals, each tied to a fragment of the Keeper's power. Their success at the mountain shrine had only scratched the surface of the task before them.

As they reached the forest edge, Yamato slowed his pace. His sword hung limply at his side, its blade nicked and dulled from the fight. The adrenaline that had fueled him earlier was gone, replaced by an aching weariness. He looked at his friends. Riku walked with his sword slung over his shoulder, his usual confidence replaced by a grim expression. Aiko nursed a sprained wrist, her movements slower than usual. Haru trudged along, silent and alert as ever, scanning the shadows for any sign of danger.

"We should rest," Yamato finally said, breaking the silence. "The Keeper is weakened, but it won't stay that way for long."

Sana nodded, glancing back at the orb. "We need to regroup and plan our next move. The orb will take time to recharge before it can guide us to the next seal."

They set up camp in a clearing, the faint light of the orb providing a sense of security in the oppressive darkness. As they sat around the fire, Sana spread a map across the ground. She pointed to a series of ancient symbols etched into the parchment.

"The next seal is far to the west, beyond the Black Marshes," she said. "It's the most remote and dangerous of them all, but it holds the Keeper's largest fragment. If we can activate it, we'll weaken the Keeper significantly."

Aiko frowned, her voice laced with concern. "The Black Marshes are cursed. People who go there don't come back."

"We don't have a choice," Sana replied. "If the Keeper gets to that seal before we do, it will be unstoppable."

The group exchanged uneasy glances. They had faced the Keeper once and barely survived. The thought of venturing into a place as perilous as the Black Marshes was daunting, but they knew the stakes.

As the fire crackled, Yamato felt a strange unease settle over him. The forest was too quiet, as though the world itself was holding its breath. He tightened his grip on his sword and scanned the shadows beyond the camp.

And then, it came.

The ground beneath them trembled, and a chilling wind swept through the clearing, snuffing out the fire. The orb in Sana's hands flared to life, its glow pulsing wildly. The whispers returned, louder and more insistent, echoing in their minds.

"It's here," Haru said, his voice barely above a whisper.

The shadows at the edge of the clearing twisted and writhed, and the Keeper emerged. It was different this time—larger, more solid, and filled with a furious energy. Its glowing eyes burned with an intensity that made Yamato's blood run cold.

"You thought you could defeat me," the Keeper snarled, its voice a low growl. "You are fools to think you can escape my wrath."

Without warning, the Keeper struck. Its shadowy tendrils lashed out, smashing into the ground with terrifying force. The group scattered, their training and instincts kicking in. Yamato lunged forward, his sword slicing through one of the tendrils. The blade connected, but the Keeper barely flinched.

Riku charged in from the side, his sword glowing faintly with the residual energy of the seal. He slashed at the Keeper's form, each strike sending ripples through its shadowy body. "It's stronger!" he shouted. "It's feeding off the seals we haven't activated yet!"

Aiko darted around the battlefield, her movements swift and precise. She landed blow after blow, targeting the Keeper's glowing core, but it seemed to absorb the attacks without weakening.

Sana clutched the orb, her face pale and determined. "I can't activate another seal from here," she called out. "We have to draw it away!"

Haru stepped forward, his slingshot loaded with a glowing shard of stone they had taken from the mountain shrine. He fired it directly at the Keeper's eyes, the projectile exploding on impact. The creature recoiled, its form flickering as though destabilized.

"Now!" Haru shouted. "We need to move!"

The group retreated, weaving through the forest as the Keeper pursued them. Its fury was palpable, its roars shaking the very trees. Yamato pushed himself to keep moving, his legs burning with effort. He glanced back and saw the Keeper gaining on them, its shadow stretching out like a living storm.

"This way!" Sana yelled, leading them toward a narrow ravine. The path was treacherous, but it offered a chance to slow the Keeper's advance. They scrambled down the rocky slope, the sound of the Keeper's roars echoing above them.

At the bottom of the ravine, they found a narrow cave entrance, barely large enough for them to squeeze through. "Inside!" Sana urged, waving them forward.

One by one, they slipped into the cave, the Keeper's tendrils slashing at the air just behind them. The last to enter, Yamato turned and faced the entrance, his sword raised. The Keeper's form loomed outside, too large to follow. Its eyes burned with rage as it peered into the darkness.

"This is not the end," the Keeper hissed, its voice echoing like a promise. "You cannot hide forever."

With a final roar, the creature withdrew, its shadowy form melting into the night.

The group collapsed inside the cave, their breaths coming in ragged gasps. The faint glow of the orb lit the space, casting long shadows on the walls.

"We survived," Aiko said, her voice shaky.

"For now," Sana replied. "But the Keeper is learning. The next time we face it, it will be even stronger."

Yamato leaned against the wall, his sword resting on the ground beside him. The weight of their mission pressed heavily on his shoulders, but he refused to let it crush him.

"We'll find the next seal," he said, his voice steady. "And we'll stop it—no matter what it takes."

The Final Seal

The group rested briefly in the cave, their bodies worn and their spirits frayed. The faint hum of the orb was the only sound in the darkness. Yamato clenched his fists, forcing himself to stay calm. He glanced at Sana, who was studying the orb with a determined focus.

"How long until it shows us the way to the next seal?" he asked.

Sana shook her head. "Not long. But the Keeper will be waiting for us. We have to be ready for anything."

The group exchanged weary glances. They all knew what this meant. The Keeper was growing stronger, and their window to act was shrinking. If they didn't succeed this time, it would be their end—and Kirigakure's.

A faint glow pulsed from the orb, casting shimmering patterns on the cave walls. Sana's eyes widened. "It's ready," she said. "The final seal is east of here, deep in the Forgotten Ruins."

"The Forgotten Ruins?" Riku asked, his voice grim. "That place is a graveyard for warriors. No one's returned from there in decades."

"We'll return," Yamato said firmly, rising to his feet. "We have to."

The journey to the Forgotten Ruins was grueling. The landscape became harsher with each step, the air heavy with an unnatural stillness. The whispers of the Keeper returned, louder and more sinister. It was watching them, taunting them.

When they finally reached the ruins, the sight was both awe-inspiring and terrifying. Towering stone pillars jutted out of the cracked earth, covered in ancient carvings that seemed to pulse with a faint, eerie light. The ruins stretched out like a labyrinth, the air thick with an oppressive energy.

Sana held the orb tightly. "The seal is at the heart of the ruins," she said. "We'll have to move fast. The Keeper will know we're here."

As if on cue, the ground trembled, and the air filled with a low, guttural growl. Shadows coalesced at the far end of the ruins, and the Keeper emerged. Its form was more solid than ever, its glowing eyes blazing with malice.

"You have come far," the Keeper hissed, its voice reverberating through the ruins. "But this ends here. Your struggle is meaningless."

Yamato drew his sword, his heart pounding. "We'll see about that."

The battle erupted with terrifying force. The Keeper attacked with relentless fury, its tendrils smashing through stone and earth. Yamato and Riku charged forward, their blades glowing faintly with the energy of the previous seals. Each strike sent ripples through the Keeper's form, but it fought back with even greater ferocity.

Aiko darted through the ruins, using her agility to land precise strikes on the Keeper's core. Haru fired glowing shards from his slingshot, each hit disrupting the creature's movements. Sana stayed back, clutching the orb as it began to glow brighter.

"I need time to activate the seal!" Sana shouted.

"We'll buy you that time!" Yamato called back, dodging a tendril that smashed into the ground where he had stood moments earlier.

The Keeper roared, its form shifting and expanding. Shadows spilled out of it like a living storm, enveloping the ruins. The group fought with everything they had, their movements sharp and precise despite their exhaustion.

But the Keeper was relentless. It struck Riku with a tendril, sending him crashing into a stone pillar. Aiko was nearly caught in the blast, but Haru pulled her back just in time.

"We can't hold it off much longer!" Haru yelled.

The orb in Sana's hands pulsed violently, its light now almost blinding. The ground beneath them began to glow with intricate symbols, the energy of the final seal coming to life.

"It's ready!" Sana cried. "Get to the center!"

Yamato led the charge, his sword blazing as he cut a path through the shadows. The group converged at the center of the ruins, where the orb's energy connected with the ancient carvings. A massive circle of light erupted from the ground, encasing the Keeper in its glow.

The creature screamed, its form writhing as the seal's power began to pull it apart. "You cannot defeat me!" it roared, its voice a mix of rage and desperation. "I am eternal!"

The group stood firm, their eyes locked on the Keeper as the seal's light grew brighter and brighter.

"This is the end for you!" Yamato shouted, raising his sword. "Your reign of terror is over!"

With a final, deafening roar, the Keeper's form was sucked into the seal. The light consumed it entirely, and then, all at once, the ruins fell silent.

The group stood in stunned silence, their breaths heavy and their bodies trembling. The glowing orb in Sana's hands dimmed, its energy completely spent. The carvings on the ground faded, leaving behind only faint traces of the battle that had just taken place.

"It's over," Sana whispered, her voice filled with a mixture of relief and exhaustion.

Yamato lowered his sword, his gaze sweeping over his friends. They were battered and bruised, but alive. He allowed himself a small, weary smile.

"We did it," he said.

As they left the ruins, the oppressive energy that had hung over the land began to lift. The sky brightened, and the air felt lighter. They had succeeded in sealing the Keeper's power, bringing peace back to Kirigakure and the world beyond.

But in the back of Yamato's mind, he couldn't shake a lingering feeling. The Keeper's final words echoed in his thoughts: *I am eternal.*

For now, the world was safe. But Yamato knew that if the Keeper ever returned, they would be ready. Together, they had faced the impossible and won—and they would do it again if they had to.

CHAPTER TWO

RISE OF THE SPECTER

Kirigakure's peace was short-lived. After defeating the Keeper, the villagers thought they were finally safe, but strange events began to unfold. Shadows started moving on their own, creeping along walls even when the sun was high in the sky. Animals vanished from farms overnight, leaving no tracks. And most unsettling of all, the days grew darker, with the sun setting earlier than it should.

Yamato felt uneasy. He hadn't been able to shake the Keeper's final words: *"I am eternal."* He couldn't explain it, but something in the air felt wrong. He spent his days training harder than ever, preparing for a danger he couldn't yet name.

One evening, as he and Aiko patrolled the outskirts of the village, they noticed something strange in the distance. A massive black cloud loomed on the horizon. At first, Yamato thought it was just a storm, but then he saw it moving—against the wind. The dark mass crept closer to the village, slow but deliberate.

"That's not normal," Aiko said, gripping her daggers tightly.

Yamato nodded, his hand resting on the hilt of his sword. "Stay alert. We don't know what we're dealing with."

The cloud stopped just beyond the village's borders, swirling and crackling with purple lightning. From its center, a figure began to take shape. At first, it was nothing but a shadow, but as the lightning flickered, the figure became clearer. It was tall and imposing, covered in sleek black armor that seemed to shimmer like liquid metal. Its face was hidden behind a jagged mask, and glowing purple eyes stared out from the darkness.

The figure stepped forward, its heavy boots crunching against the earth. The air around it grew colder, and a deep, rumbling voice echoed across the fields.

"I am Kael," it said. "The Specter of the Void. You defeated the Keeper, but that was only the beginning. I have come to finish what it started."

The villagers who had gathered to watch the spectacle screamed and scattered as Kael raised one armored hand. Dark energy surged from his palm, striking the ground and leaving a smoldering crater. Yamato and Aiko stood their ground, weapons drawn.

"Who are you? What do you want?" Yamato demanded, stepping forward.

Kael tilted his head, his glowing eyes fixed on Yamato. "What I *want* is irrelevant. The void hungers, and I am its harbinger. Your world will fall, just as countless others have before it."

Before Yamato could respond, Kael unleashed another wave of energy. The blast was so powerful that it sent both Yamato and Aiko flying back, their weapons knocked from their hands. When Yamato scrambled to his feet, Kael was gone, leaving only scorched earth and the lingering chill of his presence.

Back at the elder's hall, Yamato and the others gathered to discuss what had happened. The villagers were terrified, and rumors of Kael's power spread like wildfire. Sana laid a piece of charred stone on the table, its surface covered in glowing purple symbols. She had collected it from the site of Kael's appearance and was now studying it intently.

"This is void magic," Sana said, her voice trembling slightly. "These symbols... they're ancient. Kael isn't just a powerful enemy—he's connected to the same darkness that gave the Keeper its power. But Kael is stronger. He doesn't need seals or rituals to grow stronger. He draws his power directly from the void itself."

"So how do we stop him?" Riku asked, his usually confident voice uncertain.

Sana shook her head. "I don't know. The void isn't something you can fight like a normal enemy. It's endless. If we're going to have any chance, we need more information."

Yamato leaned forward, his expression determined. "Then we find it. There must be something—an ancient text, a lost artifact, anything that can give us a way to fight back."

Riku suddenly spoke up. "The Forbidden Archives," he said.

Everyone turned to him. "What are the Forbidden Archives?" Aiko asked.

"It's a hidden library," Riku explained. "Guarded by the Order of Ash. They're scholars who've been collecting knowledge for centuries—especially knowledge about dark magic and the void. If anyone knows how to stop Kael, it's them."

Sana frowned. "The Order of Ash doesn't trust outsiders. They won't just hand over their secrets."

"They don't have to trust us," Yamato said firmly. "They just need to see that Kael is a threat to everyone. If we explain what's at stake, they'll help us."

The group agreed, though they knew the journey to the archives wouldn't be easy. The Forbidden Archives were said to be deep in the Wailing Mountains, a treacherous range where the winds howled so fiercely that they drowned out even the loudest cries for help.

The road to the archives was as dangerous as they had feared. As they traveled, the land seemed to grow darker, the sky permanently overcast. They were attacked by shadow beasts—creatures that seemed to rise out of the very ground itself. Yamato and the others fought bravely, their weapons glowing faintly with the energy of the seals they had gathered during their battle with the Keeper.

But the shadow beasts were relentless, and the group grew more exhausted with each passing day. By the time they reached the base of the Wailing Mountains, their clothes were torn, and their bodies ached from the constant fighting.

At the top of the mountain, they found the gates to the Forbidden Archives. Massive and carved from stone, the gates were covered in glowing runes. Standing in front of them was a woman with sharp eyes and silver hair, wearing robes embroidered with fiery patterns. She looked at the group with suspicion.

"I am Eira, leader of the Order of Ash," she said. "Why do you bring the stench of void magic to our gates?"

Yamato stepped forward, meeting her gaze. "We don't want to, but we have no choice. Kael, the Specter of the Void, is coming. He's already attacked Kirigakure, and he won't stop there. If we don't find a way to stop him, the void will consume everything."

Eira studied him for a long moment before finally nodding. "If what you say is true, you'll need all the help you can get. But be warned—the answers you seek may be more dangerous than the enemy you face."

The stone gates of the Forbidden Archives creaked open, revealing a dark, echoing corridor lined with flickering torches. The air inside was cool and heavy, as if the weight of centuries pressed down on it. Yamato and the others followed Eira in silence, their footsteps soft against the smooth stone floor.

"Stay close," Eira warned. "The archives are vast, and not all knowledge here is meant to be touched. The wrong scroll or artifact could doom you faster than Kael ever could."

They entered a massive hall, its walls towering high and packed with shelves of books, scrolls, and strange glowing artifacts. In the center stood a grand table carved from obsidian, its surface etched with shifting runes that seemed alive. Eira gestured for them to sit as she unfurled a map.

"This is the knowledge we've gathered about the void," she said, pointing to a section marked with dark symbols. "The void is endless, but its power flows through conduits—anchors that tie it to this world. The Keeper was one such anchor, but Kael... he is different. He is not just a servant of the void—he has become its vessel."

Sana leaned forward, her brow furrowed. "If Kael is the vessel, then how do we stop him? Destroy the vessel?"

Eira's gaze hardened. "Destroying Kael might not be enough. The void will simply choose another. If you want to stop him permanently, you must sever his connection to the void."

"And how do we do that?" Riku asked.

Eira hesitated, then pointed to a section of the map labeled *The Shattered Nexus*. "This is where you must go. The Nexus is an ancient site, older than even the archives. It is said to be a point where the void touches our world. If you can disrupt the Nexus, you can cut Kael's connection to the void."

Yamato frowned. "That sounds simple enough. What's the catch?"

Eira smirked faintly. "The catch is that no one has ever returned from the Nexus. It is guarded by void-born creatures far more powerful than anything you've faced. And even if you reach the Nexus, you'll need a relic to activate its power."

She turned and opened a small, locked chest on a nearby shelf. Inside was a jagged, black crystal glowing faintly with purple light. "This is the Voidshard," she said. "It's the only thing capable of activating the Nexus. But using it is dangerous. Its power can corrupt even the strongest mind."

Sana reached out to touch the shard, but Eira grabbed her wrist. "Do not touch it until the time is right," she said sharply. "Its energy could destroy you if you're not prepared."

Yamato took the shard carefully, wrapping it in cloth before placing it in his satchel. "We'll take the risk," he said firmly. "If this is the only way to stop Kael, we don't have a choice."

Eira looked at them, her expression unreadable. "I hope you're ready," she said. "Because once you leave this place, the void will know what you're planning. And it will do everything in its power to stop you."

The group left the archives with a renewed sense of purpose but also a growing unease. The weight of their mission pressed heavily on them, and the journey ahead felt more perilous than anything they had faced before.

As they descended the mountain, the sky grew darker, and an unnatural silence fell over the land. It was as if the void itself was watching them.

Suddenly, the ground shook violently, and a piercing screech echoed through the air. From the shadows of the forest, monstrous creatures emerged—void beasts unlike any they had seen before. These were larger, faster, and more ferocious, their forms shifting constantly as if they couldn't decide what shape to take.

"Prepare yourselves!" Yamato shouted, drawing his sword.

The battle was fierce. Yamato and Riku fought side by side, their blades glowing faintly with the lingering energy of the Keeper's seals. Aiko darted between the creatures, her daggers striking with deadly precision, while Haru fired glowing bolts from his slingshot.

But the void beasts were relentless. One of them lunged at Sana, its claws outstretched. She barely managed to dodge, stumbling as she tried to channel a spell. Yamato saw her struggle and rushed to her side, slicing through the beast just before it reached her.

"Stay focused!" he yelled.

"I'm trying!" Sana replied, her hands trembling as she formed a glowing barrier around the group.

The creatures pressed closer, their attacks growing more coordinated. It was as if they were being controlled by a single mind. Yamato realized they couldn't win this fight—not like this.

"We have to move!" he shouted. "Sana, can you hold them off long enough for us to escape?"

Sana nodded, sweat dripping down her face. "I'll try."

She raised her hands, and a dome of shimmering light surrounded them. The void beasts clawed at it, but the barrier held—for now. The group ran, the sounds of the beasts' screeches fading as they put more distance between themselves and the battle.

When they finally stopped to catch their breath, Sana collapsed to her knees, exhausted.

"They're not going to stop," she said weakly. "They'll keep coming until we reach the Nexus."

Yamato helped her to her feet. "Then we won't stop either," he said firmly. "We'll reach the Nexus, and we'll end this. Together."

As they pressed on, the weight of the Voidshard in Yamato's satchel seemed to grow heavier with each step. The journey ahead was dark and uncertain, but they knew one thing for sure—Kael and the void weren't going to wait for them. The final battle was drawing closer, and the fate of their world hung in the balance.

The group trekked through the desolate landscape, their steps quickened by the ever-present sense of danger. The forest had long since given way to barren wastelands, the air thick with the stench of decay. The land seemed to reject life itself, the void's corruption spreading like a dark plague.

Yamato adjusted the Voidshard in his satchel, its faint hum growing louder with each passing hour. He could feel its presence more clearly now, as if it were alive and aware of their intentions.

"How much farther?" Aiko asked, her voice tense.

"Not far," Sana replied, clutching the map Eira had given them. "The Shattered Nexus is just beyond that ridge."

As they climbed, the wind picked up, carrying whispers that sent chills down their spines. Yamato recognized the voices—the same ones that had haunted them since they first confronted the Keeper. But now, they were stronger, more insistent.

"You cannot win," the whispers hissed. "The void is eternal. You are nothing."

"Shut up," Riku muttered, gripping his sword tightly.

At the top of the ridge, they froze. Below them stretched the Shattered Nexus, a massive crater surrounded by jagged rocks and swirling shadows. In the center stood a towering obelisk, its surface covered in glowing void runes. The air crackled with dark energy, and the ground pulsed like a heartbeat.

"It's worse than I imagined," Sana said, her voice barely audible.

The group descended carefully, the oppressive energy of the Nexus growing stronger with each step. As they neared the obelisk, the shadows around it began to shift and coalesce, forming a tall, humanoid figure cloaked in darkness.

Kael.

He stepped forward, his glowing eyes locked on Yamato. His voice was deep and resonant, filled with a calm malice. "You've come far, but it's over now. The Nexus is beyond your comprehension. You cannot sever what was never meant to be broken."

Yamato stepped forward, drawing his sword. "We'll see about that."

Kael laughed, a sound that seemed to reverberate through the entire crater. "Brave words, but futile. The void flows through me. I am its vessel, its will. And you..." He gestured to the group. "You are insects, scurrying in the dark."

Without warning, Kael raised his hand, and the ground beneath them erupted. Tendrils of shadow shot toward the group, forcing them to scatter. Yamato rolled to the side, narrowly avoiding a strike, and charged at Kael, his blade glowing with faint light.

Kael met Yamato's attack with a wave of dark energy, sending him flying backward. "You cannot defeat me with brute strength," Kael said, advancing. "The void is limitless. Your power is a flicker of light in an endless sea of darkness."

Sana raised her hands, chanting a spell. A beam of light shot from her palms, striking Kael and momentarily halting his advance. But Kael absorbed the energy, the runes on his body glowing brighter.

"Pathetic," he sneered, unleashing a blast of energy that shattered Sana's barrier.

Aiko and Riku flanked Kael, attacking from either side. Aiko's daggers struck with precision, while Riku's blade clashed against Kael's shadow-forged weapon. Haru fired bolts of light from his slingshot, each one aimed at the runes on Kael's body.

Kael countered with ease, his movements fluid and deliberate. "You fight well, but it's meaningless. The Nexus will devour you all."

Yamato struggled to his feet, his body aching. He reached for the Voidshard, feeling its immense power thrumming through the cloth. "Sana! How do we use this?" he called out.

Sana dodged another of Kael's attacks, her voice strained. "You have to place it on the obelisk! It's the only way to disrupt the Nexus!"

Yamato nodded, gripping the shard tightly. He charged toward the obelisk, but Kael appeared in his path, his shadowy form blocking the way.

"Foolish boy," Kael said, his voice cold. "Do you really think you can stop me?"

Yamato's grip tightened on his sword. "I don't think. I act."

With a burst of speed, Yamato feinted to the left, then rolled to the right, narrowly avoiding Kael's strike. He sprinted toward the obelisk, the Voidshard glowing brighter in his hand.

Kael roared in anger, the shadows around him lashing out wildly. Riku and Aiko dove in, their attacks aimed at Kael's core, buying Yamato precious seconds.

As Yamato reached the obelisk, the shard's glow intensified, its energy merging with the void runes. The air around him grew heavy, and the ground beneath his feet trembled. He slammed the Voidshard into the obelisk, and a blinding light erupted from the Nexus.

Kael screamed, his form flickering as the light consumed him. The shadows retreated, swirling chaotically before dissipating into nothingness.

"It's working!" Sana shouted, shielding her eyes from the light.

The obelisk began to crack, its surface splitting apart as the Nexus's energy spiraled out of control. The ground quaked violently, and the group scrambled to retreat.

Yamato turned to see Kael's form disintegrating, his voice a mix of rage and desperation. "This isn't over!" Kael roared. "The void will find another! You cannot escape its grasp!"

With a final, deafening explosion, the obelisk shattered, and the Nexus collapsed in on itself, leaving only silence in its wake.

The group stood on the edge of the crater, their bodies battered and their breaths heavy. The oppressive energy of the void was gone, replaced by a strange stillness.

"It's over," Yamato said, though his voice was tinged with uncertainty.

But in the back of his mind, he couldn't shake Kael's final words. The void's grip may have loosened, but had it truly been severed?

For now, the world was safe, and the group allowed themselves a moment of relief. But they knew that the void was a force beyond understanding—and its shadow might one day return.

The group stood silently at the edge of the shattered crater. The land, once suffocated by the void's power, now seemed lifeless and eerily quiet. A faint breeze brushed past them, carrying the ashes of the fallen obelisk.

Yamato glanced down at the Voidshard, now dull and cracked in his hands. Its once-threatening hum was gone, leaving only a faint vibration, like the last breath of a dying flame.

"Is it really over?" Aiko asked, her voice breaking the silence.

"I don't know," Yamato said honestly. He looked at Sana, who was kneeling on the ground, inspecting the remnants of the void runes.

Sana shook her head. "The Nexus is gone, and Kael is defeated. But this shard..." She pointed at the Voidshard. "It's not fully destroyed. That means the void might still have a link to our world."

Riku groaned, wiping sweat from his forehead. "Great. So, we nearly died for nothing?"

Haru, leaning on his slingshot, shrugged. "At least the Keeper's power is gone. That's got to count for something, right?"

Yamato didn't reply. His eyes were fixed on the horizon, where the faint outlines of the forest they'd crossed earlier were visible. Something about the stillness of the air didn't feel right.

"Let's get back to Kirigakure," Yamato said, breaking the uneasy moment. "We need to regroup and figure out our next steps."

The journey back was slow and exhausting. The group moved carefully, their injuries from the fight with Kael slowing them down. Sana carried the broken Voidshard, wrapped in cloth to keep its unsettling energy contained.

As they entered the forest, the atmosphere seemed lighter. The oppressive whispers of the void were gone, and sunlight filtered through the trees. But even with the absence of darkness, Yamato's instincts told him not to relax.

When they reached Kirigakure, the villagers greeted them with cautious hope. Many had felt the shift in the land when the Nexus collapsed and came out of hiding. Yamato noticed the relief on their faces, but he also saw fear in their eyes. They knew this wasn't the end.

The group headed straight to Eira's cottage. The old seer was waiting for them, her expression unreadable. As they entered, she gestured for them to sit around the low table.

"You succeeded," Eira said simply, her voice heavy.

"Kind of," Yamato replied, placing the damaged Voidshard on the table. "The Nexus is destroyed, but this thing isn't. Kael said the void would find another way."

Eira's eyes narrowed as she studied the shard. "The void is persistent. It is not just a force but a will. Severing one connection may not stop it entirely."

Aiko crossed her arms. "Then what are we supposed to do? Fight another Kael? Another Keeper?"

Eira looked at each of them, her gaze filled with both pride and concern. "The void feeds on fear, despair, and imbalance. As long as such emotions exist, it will seek a way into our world. But you are not without hope. Together, you've proven that even against overwhelming darkness, light can prevail."

"That's not really comforting," Riku muttered, earning a sharp elbow from Aiko.

Eira continued. "The shard is weak now, but its energy must be contained. If it falls into the wrong hands..." She didn't finish, but the meaning was clear.

"Then we'll guard it," Yamato said firmly. "We'll make sure no one uses it again."

Eira nodded but seemed hesitant. "There is another matter," she said. "I've felt a disturbance—a new presence that arrived the moment the Nexus fell."

The group exchanged uneasy glances.

"What kind of presence?" Haru asked.

Eira leaned forward, her voice dropping. "A powerful one. Not of the void, but not of this world either. It moves with purpose, searching for something—or someone."

Yamato felt a chill run down his spine. "Do you think it's connected to the void?"

"It's possible," Eira admitted. "Or it could be something else entirely. But whatever it is, it's heading this way."

The room fell silent. The group had barely recovered from their fight with Kael, and now a new threat was already on the horizon.

"We need to be ready," Sana said, breaking the tension. "If this thing is coming here, we can't let it catch us off guard."

Riku stood, gripping his sword. "Guess there's no time to rest, huh?"

Yamato rose as well, determination hardening in his eyes. "We've faced the void and survived. Whatever this new enemy is, we'll deal with it the same way. Together."

Eira smiled faintly. "Good. Because the winds of fate are shifting, and your roles in this story are far from over."

Outside, the first stars began to appear in the night sky. But to Yamato, the darkness seemed deeper than usual, as if the void had left behind a shadow that refused to fade.

As they prepared for what lay ahead, Yamato couldn't help but wonder: was this just the

The air in Kirigakure grew colder overnight. The once-calm village now felt tense, as if the land itself was holding its breath. The faint whispers of villagers were laced with fear as they gathered around small fires, sharing rumors about what might come next.

Yamato and his team stayed close to Eira's cottage, preparing for the unknown threat the seer had warned them about. The Voidshard rested on the table, wrapped tightly in layers of cloth.

Even in its weakened state, its presence was unsettling, radiating a faint, eerie pulse.

"We need a plan," Sana said, breaking the uneasy silence. "If this new enemy reaches Kirigakure, we can't just wait for it to attack."

"I agree," Yamato said. "But we don't even know what we're dealing with. We need more information."

Eira nodded, her expression grim. "I've been meditating on its presence. Whatever it is, it is not bound by the laws of this world. It moves like a shadow but strikes with precision. It seeks something specific—something tied to the Voidshard."

"Then we need to move the shard," Riku said. "If it's coming for that, we can't let it stay here."

Haru shook his head. "And take it where? Anywhere we go, it'll just follow us. At least here, we have the village to help defend."

Yamato clenched his fists. "No. We can't risk the village. Too many people would get caught in the crossfire. We'll face this thing outside Kirigakure."

Aiko, who had been unusually quiet, finally spoke. "What if it's not coming for the shard?" she asked. "What if it's coming for... us?"

The room fell silent. The weight of her words settled heavily on everyone.

"Then we face it head-on," Yamato said after a moment, his voice steady. "We've dealt with the void before. This won't be any different."

But deep down, Yamato wasn't so sure.

At dawn, the group left Kirigakure, taking the Voidshard with them. They traveled north, toward an open plain surrounded by jagged cliffs. It was a place where they could see their enemy coming and avoid endangering anyone else.

The journey was eerily quiet. The usual sounds of birds and rustling leaves were absent, replaced by an oppressive stillness. Even the wind felt unnatural, cold and biting despite the rising sun.

"Does anyone else feel like we're being watched?" Aiko whispered, glancing over her shoulder.

"You're not imagining it," Sana replied, her hand gripping the orb that had guided them through so many trials before. "The energy in the air... it's similar to the void, but different. More focused."

As they reached the cliffs, Yamato motioned for the group to stop. He scanned the horizon, his senses on high alert.

"Anything?" Riku asked, gripping his sword tightly.

"Not yet," Yamato said. "But it's close. I can feel it."

Suddenly, the ground beneath them began to tremble. A low, guttural sound echoed across the plain, sending chills down their spines. The sky darkened, as if a storm was forming, but there were no clouds—just an unnatural shadow creeping over the land.

And then, it appeared.

At first, it was nothing more than a shifting mass of darkness, swirling and pulsing like liquid smoke. But as it drew closer, it began to take shape. A tall figure emerged, cloaked in shadows that seemed to ripple like fire. Its face was hidden beneath a jagged mask, and its eyes glowed a deep, malevolent crimson.

The group instinctively formed a defensive circle, weapons at the ready.

"So, this is the one Eira warned us about," Riku muttered. "Great. It looks even worse than I imagined."

The figure stopped a few meters away, its presence suffocating. When it spoke, its voice was a chilling blend of whispers and echoes, as if it came from every direction at once.

"You bear the shard," it said, its words slicing through the air. "The void's will lingers within it. Surrender it to me, and I may let you live."

Yamato stepped forward, his sword glowing faintly with the energy of the seals they had activated before. "Who are you? Why do you want the shard?"

The figure tilted its head slightly, as if amused. "I am the Phantom—a harbinger of balance. The shard disrupts the order of this world. It must be returned to the void, or chaos will consume all."

"Yeah, we've heard that one before," Aiko said, rolling her eyes. "You're not getting it."

The Phantom's crimson eyes narrowed. "Then you have chosen death."

Without warning, it attacked. Tendrils of shadow shot out from its body, slamming into the ground with explosive force. Yamato and the others scattered, dodging the assault.

Yamato lunged forward, his blade cutting through one of the tendrils. The shadow dissolved, but more took its place, twisting and striking with incredible speed.

"Stay together!" Yamato shouted, blocking another attack. "We can't let it separate us!"

Riku and Aiko flanked the Phantom, their movements synchronized. Riku's sword clashed with the Phantom's tendrils while Aiko darted in and out, landing quick, precise strikes. Haru fired glowing projectiles from his slingshot, aiming for the Phantom's core.

But the Phantom was fast—almost impossibly so. It moved with a fluid grace, avoiding most of their attacks while countering with devastating precision.

Sana stood at the edge of the battle, clutching the orb tightly. She focused on the shard's energy, trying to find a way to use it against the Phantom. "I need more time!" she called out.

"We'll give you as much as we can!" Yamato replied, slashing through another tendril.

The battle raged on, each strike shaking the ground beneath them. Despite their efforts, the Phantom seemed unfazed, its shadowy form regenerating as quickly as they could damage it.

"It's too strong!" Riku yelled. "We need a plan!"

Yamato gritted his teeth, his mind racing. They had faced impossible odds before, but this felt different. The Phantom wasn't just powerful—it was deliberate, calculating, and utterly relentless.

As the Phantom loomed over them, its crimson eyes burning brighter, Yamato realized one thing:

Yamato's mind raced as he dodged another strike from the Phantom's tendrils. They couldn't just keep fighting like this; they were running out of time, and their energy was draining. His eyes flicked toward Sana, who was still trying to focus on the orb.

"Sana!" he shouted. "Is there anything you can do with the shard? Anything that can stop it?"

Sana's eyes were narrowed in concentration, sweat beading on her forehead. "I... I'm trying, but it's fighting me," she replied, her voice strained. "The Phantom's energy is intertwined with the shard. It's not just a force of darkness—it's tied to the very fabric of the void. If I can't sever the connection, we'll never defeat it!"

Yamato's heart sank. They needed to end this now. But how?

The Phantom loomed in front of them again, its form shifting like smoke. "Your resistance is futile," it said, its voice cold and full of contempt. "You cannot stop what was meant to be. The void will reclaim this world, and there is nothing you can do to change that."

Aiko, already winded, turned to Yamato. "We can't hold it off much longer. What do we do?"

Yamato clenched his sword. He couldn't afford to lose. Not after everything they had gone through.

Then, it came to him.

"Riku, Aiko," Yamato said, his voice steady. "I need you to focus on keeping the Phantom distracted. I have a plan."

Riku raised an eyebrow. "A plan? You've got something up your sleeve, don't you?"

"I hope so," Yamato replied, nodding toward the orb. "Sana, you need to hold the shard steady, but I'll need you to sync with me when I say so. We have one chance."

Sana didn't question him. She simply nodded, her hands tightening around the orb.

The Phantom let out an eerie laugh as it loomed over them. "You think you can outsmart me? Foolish children."

As it swung its tendrils toward them, Riku and Aiko darted forward, drawing the Phantom's attention. They fought with everything they had, Riku blocking tendrils while Aiko made quick strikes.

Yamato didn't waste any more time. He rushed forward, closing the distance between him and the Phantom. He needed to get close enough to land a decisive blow, but the creature's shadows swirled around him, making it difficult to see.

Then, Yamato saw it—the Phantom's weakness. There was a faint, pulsing glow at its core, right where the energy from the Voidshard seemed to concentrate. That was where he needed to strike.

With his sword raised, he charged at the Phantom's center, pushing through the swirling tendrils. He could feel the darkness pressing in on him, trying to pull him under. But he focused only on that glow.

He reached the Phantom's core and swung his blade with all his might, connecting with the glowing center. The Phantom let out an ear-piercing screech as the sword cut through its essence. For a moment, the creature seemed to freeze in place, its form faltering.

At that exact moment, Sana activated the orb, its light flaring bright. The energy from the Voidshard exploded outward, creating a pulse of power that wrapped around the Phantom.

The Phantom roared in agony, its body convulsing as the light overwhelmed it. Tendrils whipped violently, smashing into the ground as the core cracked open.

But just as quickly as it began, the Phantom's form started to disintegrate. Shadowy fragments scattered into the air, dissolving into nothingness.

For a brief moment, there was silence.

Then, the group let out collective breaths, their exhaustion catching up to them all at once. Yamato lowered his sword, his body shaking with relief. He glanced at his friends, his team.

"We did it," Riku said, his voice full of disbelief.

"We actually did it," Aiko added, wiping sweat from her brow.

Sana, though exhausted, smiled faintly. "The shard's energy... It's fading. We've stopped the connection, at least for now."

Yamato turned his gaze toward the horizon. The sky, once darkened by the Phantom's presence, was starting to brighten again. The oppressive weight that had hung over the land was lifting, and for the first time in what felt like ages, the air felt lighter.

But even as the group stood victorious, Yamato couldn't shake the feeling that something was still off.

"We've won for now," Yamato said, his voice quiet but firm. "But this won't be the last time we face an enemy like this. The void won't give up so easily."

Sana nodded in agreement, holding the Voidshard tightly. "You're right. This battle might be over, but the war isn't. We have to stay prepared."

As they stood there, watching the last remnants of the Phantom fade into the wind, they knew that their fight was far from over. The world was changing, and new threats would rise. But Yamato and his friends were ready to face whatever came next—together.

The group began to walk away from the site of the battle, each step heavy with exhaustion. Yamato could feel the weight of the world pressing down on him again. The victory they had just won was important, yes, but it felt like the calm before another storm. As they made their way back to their camp, the skies cleared, revealing a full moon rising in the distance. It was beautiful, but even its light seemed eerie after everything that had happened.

"We should rest," Sana suggested, her voice soft. "We need to regain our strength. The energy from the orb has drained us, and we don't know what else might be out there."

Riku stretched, still feeling the burn from the battle. "I'll take the first watch. You all get some sleep. I'll wake you if anything happens."

Yamato nodded. "Good idea. We'll need to be ready in case there's another surprise waiting for us."

As the group set up camp for the night, Yamato found himself unable to rest. His thoughts kept swirling, focusing on the Phantom's final words: *I am eternal.* Those words kept echoing in his mind, a reminder that no matter what they had faced, this fight was far from over.

He sat away from the campfire, staring into the dark expanse of the forest. His sword rested on his knee, his fingers tracing the hilt absentmindedly.

"Sana," he said quietly, not wanting to disturb the others. "Do you think we truly defeated the Phantom? Or was this just the beginning of something worse?"

Sana sat down next to him, looking thoughtful. "I don't know. There's a darkness in the world, something old and powerful. The Phantom was just one piece of it. But even if it's gone for now, we've seen enough to know that this fight isn't over. Something is still out there."

Yamato clenched his fists, his heart heavy with uncertainty. They had just faced a terrifying creature born from the depths of the void, but that wasn't the only danger lurking in the shadows. The world felt unstable, and he could sense the ripple of something even bigger.

"We need to keep moving forward," he said, his voice resolute. "If there's more out there, we have to find it before it finds us. We can't let this darkness spread any further."

Sana nodded in agreement, her face serious. "We will. But for tonight, we rest. Tomorrow, we'll figure out our next move."

Yamato didn't feel like resting. His instincts told him that if they stayed here too long, they might become sitting targets. But he didn't want to argue. The others needed this time to recover, and so did he.

As the night wore on, the sounds of the forest grew quiet. The only noise was the occasional crackle of the campfire. Yamato sat there for hours, staring at the sky. The moonlight washed over the landscape, peaceful and calm, but in his heart, he knew the peace wouldn't last.

Suddenly, he felt a shift in the air, a coldness that made his spine tingle. It wasn't the Phantom. This was something different.

Without warning, a figure stepped out from the shadows of the trees. It was cloaked in black, its face hidden in the folds of its hood.

Yamato's hand instinctively gripped his sword, ready to spring into action. The figure didn't move, but its presence sent a wave of unease through the group.

Sana stood up slowly, her eyes narrowing. "Who are you?" she asked, her voice firm.

The figure's voice was cold and smooth, like ice scraping across stone. "I am the one who has been watching. You have no idea what you've just done."

Yamato's grip tightened on his sword. "Who are you? And what do you mean by that?"

The figure chuckled softly, the sound sending chills down Yamato's back. "You've sealed away a small part of the darkness. But the darkness will never be truly gone. It will always find a way to return. And when it does, you will not be ready."

Yamato's heart raced. He wasn't sure if this was a friend or a foe, but something about the way the figure spoke made him uneasy.

The figure raised its hand, and suddenly, the ground beneath their feet began to crack. A dark energy pulsed from the figure's fingers, swirling in the air like a storm.

"I've been watching you, Yamato," the figure said, its voice laced with malice. "And I know what you're capable of. But even you cannot stop what is coming. You will fall, just like the others."

With that, the figure stepped back into the shadows, disappearing as quickly as it had appeared.

Yamato stood frozen, his mind reeling from what he had just heard. The sense of foreboding was overwhelming. Who was that? And what did they mean by "the others"?

Sana stepped forward, her face pale. "This isn't over. There's someone or something else out there—something even more dangerous than the Phantom. We need to find it before it finds us."

Yamato nodded, his mind racing. He had a feeling that this was just the beginning of a much larger conflict. The world was far from safe.

He looked at his friends, who were all now awake, their expressions filled with worry. They could feel it too—the danger that loomed just out of sight.

"We need to prepare," Yamato said, his voice determined. "Whatever is out there, we'll face it together. But we need to move fast."

The team nodded, rallying around him. They weren't sure what the future held, but they knew one thing for certain: they would fight to the end. Whatever was coming, they would face it head-on, no matter the cost.

As the figure vanished into the shadows, the group stood in stunned silence. The night air grew colder, and the unsettling feeling of being watched never left them. Yamato's grip on his sword tightened, and he could sense the others' unease. They had just fought the Phantom, but now a new threat had emerged—one even more powerful and mysterious.

"We have to keep moving," Yamato said, breaking the silence. "There's no time to waste. We don't know what this new enemy is capable of, but we can't let them catch us off guard."

Sana nodded in agreement. "We need to find out who—or *what*—that was. But for now, we stay alert. We'll make camp again, but we can't afford to relax."

Riku, still slightly shaken by the sudden appearance of the cloaked figure, spoke up. "I'll take another watch. We should keep looking for any signs of danger."

Yamato gave him a brief nod. "Alright. Let's get some rest. We'll figure things out in the morning."

As the night passed, each of them took turns on watch, but sleep didn't come easily for any of them. Every rustling leaf or crackling twig seemed amplified, as if the forest itself was alive and watching. Yamato couldn't shake the feeling that something was out there, waiting. His mind raced with questions—who was that figure, and what did they mean by *"the darkness will return"*?

By morning, the group was exhausted but resolute. They packed their gear, and Sana took a final look around, making sure there were no signs of the mysterious figure's return.

"We need to find answers," she said, her tone firm. "We can't let this *thing* just slip away into the shadows. It knows about us, and it knows what we've done."

"Let's move out," Yamato said, standing tall and looking at his friends. "Together, we can face whatever comes next. We've made it this far, and we won't stop now."

The group set off toward the nearest village to gather more information. They needed to talk to the elders and anyone who might have heard of strange occurrences or the figure in black. The path was long, and the land around them grew even darker, as if the very earth knew of the evil lurking nearby.

As they walked, Riku spoke up, his voice thoughtful. "Do you think this could be the same darkness we've been fighting all along? The one that caused the Phantom?"

Yamato hesitated. It was a possibility, but he had a feeling this was something even older, something more dangerous than they could imagine. "I don't know, Riku. But I don't think it's over. I don't think we've even seen the full picture yet."

The group reached the village by evening, where they were welcomed with cautious curiosity. The villagers, upon hearing their story, seemed to grow more worried.

"There have been rumors," an elder explained, his face lined with age and wisdom. "Whispers of a figure cloaked in shadow, appearing in the night. Some say it's the one who controls the darkness. Others say it's a harbinger of doom."

Yamato frowned. This was the first real lead they had, but the answers only raised more questions. "Where can we find this figure?" he asked.

The elder's eyes darkened. "No one who has gone searching for it has returned. The figure does not stay in one place for long. It moves like the wind, and its intentions are unclear."

Sana crossed her arms. "We can't wait for it to find us. We need to go after it."

The elder looked worried. "You're strong, young ones, but even the bravest warriors have fallen to this shadow. I advise you to reconsider. There are things in this world—ancient, powerful things—that should not be disturbed."

But Yamato stood tall, his resolve clear. "We can't back down. The world depends on us."

The group left the village that evening, more determined than ever. The elder's warnings rang in their minds, but Yamato knew they had no choice. The shadow, whatever it was, couldn't be allowed to spread.

They ventured deep into the forest, following a faint trail of dark energy that seemed to pulse in the air. As they walked, the land grew increasingly desolate, the trees twisted and gnarled, and the sky above seemed heavy with dark clouds.

Hours passed without a word, each of them lost in their thoughts. Finally, as they reached the heart of the forest, they came upon an ancient ruin, overgrown with vines. The air was thick with a palpable sense of dread, and the ground beneath their feet seemed to hum with dark power.

"This is it," Sana whispered. "The source of the darkness."

Yamato stepped forward, his hand gripping the hilt of his sword. He knew that whatever lay ahead would be their greatest challenge yet.

The air grew colder, and the shadows around them seemed to stretch, pulling at the edges of their vision. Yamato's breath caught in his throat as he heard a familiar voice—low, cruel, and filled with malice.

"I have been waiting for you, Yamato."

The figure from before stepped out of the shadows once more, its form emerging from the darkness like a nightmare made real. This time, there was no mistaking it. The enemy was here. And it was more powerful than ever.

To be continued...

www.ingramcontent.com/pod-product-compliance
Lightning Source LLC
Chambersburg PA
CBHW022113150726
47990CB00003B/1347